The Gift of Magic

Archers Beach, Volume 5

Sharon Lee

Published by Sharon Lee, 2015.

The Gift of Music

Early September; the air crisping up, and the sea getting feisty.

Fall was bearing down on Archers Beach, and all the rest of Maine, too, the way Andy heard it, but you'd never tell it from the number of folks on the streets, and filling up all the hotels. Folk that'd come up from Away down Boston, and Montreal, Vermont, and New Hampshire. Places Andy'd only heard about, him being Archers Beach, all the way through.

He stood on the Pier, arms folded on the rail, guitar in its case nestled like a dog at his feet. Standing right there, he could look down and see the breakers strike the white beach and splinter into ivory foam. Turning his head just a little, and he could see straight up Archer Avenue, all busy with automobiles, and horse-drawn wagons, pedestrians, and the electric trolley just making the turn down from Portland Street.

Well, Andy thought, squinting up the hill against the September sun; it'd be winter soon enough, and the town hunkered down against the cold. Half the hotels would be closed by All Hallow's, and the rest by Thanksgiving Day. Then, it'd be the townies keeping their own company 'til April brought the owners back from their winter places in Portland or Boston. May and April, those were working months, repairing what the winter'd broke, cleaning up, and repainting 'til the town was fit for company again.

He straightened away from the rail, and stretched before reaching down to take the guitar in hand. Truth told, a crowd in town suited him fine; it was always better to play for something other than himself. It was nice to get paid, too, though—another truth told, even at the height of summer there wasn't a lot of work for Andy LaPierre.

The ballroom and the concert halls paid best, but they wanted the Big Bands, and the big acts up from New York and Atlantic City.

A fella like Andy—single fella with a guitar—not much call for him. Less even than a call for a duo—guitar and fiddle, like him and Cray tried doing.

Damn' fool thing, that'd been. That fiddle was dangerous, which they'd both known. Their mistake was in thinking they could handle it—which made them a pair of damnfools.

Fiddle'd almost killed a boy, dancing, at Fathom Five—well, no. Him and Cray'd—*they'd* almost killed the boy, it being them that'd brought the fiddle into it, knowing what it was. And—full truth told—if the boy *had* died, it would've been Andy's death. He was older and he should've been watching; he'd told Cray that he'd *be* watching.

But the fiddle—well. Say the fiddle had its own ideas.

In the end, Andy had come to himself in time, and no lasting harm was done. The boy'd wanted a bracer, and a friendly arm to lean on back to his hotel. Couple of Cray's fingers got burnt, but that wasn't worth mentioning—though Cray still did, now and then, being Cray.

Could've been worse.

It *did* put an end to the duo, though—no real loss. Cray didn't need the music, not like Andy did, and he was happy enough to go back to the marshland and tend his own potatoes.

So that left Andy—a fella and his guitar—playing fill-in, side, and early at the little places, and the speakeasies. Fathom Five, The Pearl and Coral, The Sea Nymph, The Conch—those were his usual venues. Once or twice a summer, he'd pick up a gig at one of the big hotel restaurants, wandering from table to table, playing soft, maybe crooning a little. That was fine, and the tips were good, but the big hotels didn't want the likes of Andy, not regular.

That was all right. It was the music that was important. More important than money. More important than love.

Learning that. . .that'd been a shocker. But the music—it wanted—it *needed*—to be played. It wouldn't let itself be put away to fester. The music—that was his gift, and it wasn't going to let him waste a single note of it.

So, Andy played where they'd have him, for the hat, and supper, sharing his gift, and, just by the way, healing himself.

Tonight, for instance, he was playing The Conch, seven to ten, which was longer than usual, but the sax player's wife had sent a note that he was under the weather. Meaning that he'd drunk too much coffin varnish again.

The word came to Andy's ear about the time it reached Mr. Flannagan, The Conch's barkeep and manager. That meant he was walking in the door, having given the doorman the word, guitar in hand, smoked glasses covering his eyes, before Flannagan had time to send 'round to any of the other regulars. The barkeep didn't necessarily like Andy, which was mutual, but he wasn't a man who relished putting in extra effort, either. Mr. Flannagan didn't like music, and he didn't like musicians, and one was as good as another to him.

Spying Andy, he gave a short nod and turned to draw a beer.

"You're playing straight through tonight," he said.

"Yes, sir," said Andy, nice and polite. He took the beer, and went down to the little stage to set up.

He could feel the music buzzing at the ends of his fingers and in-between his ears. He'd just played two days ago, but the music was eager, like there was something special brewing.

He thought about that, tuning up. Something *special*, was it? Well, if that was the case, then it had to be the night was somehow special, 'cause it sure wasn't the gig.

The Conch wasn't one of your upscale places, like the Sea Change or the Casino. But it wasn't just a townie joint, either. Flannagan didn't like townies any more than he liked music or musicians. About the only thing he *did* like was that money from Away. That being so, The Conch made itself agreeable to those folks from Away who had money, but who didn't necessarily expect the digs to be top-notch.

That meant it drew a younger crowd. A tougher crowd. Sometimes, things happened at the Conch that shouldn't've. Flannagan paid a nice percentage of that Away money to the cops, to make sure those things never came to their official notice.

Andy didn't mind the crowd; trouble never came to him that way—and hardly ever came to The Conch when he was playing. The only thing that mattered was that he got to play. Mostly, too, he played for himself; the crowd had their own business, and the sounds he made were background, or less, to them.

That was all right, too; the music did its work. It didn't have to be heard; it only had to be played.

#

He noticed them about half-way through his second set: A couple like any other from Away who owned the kind of money that would make Flannagan's nose twitch. She was pretty, he thought; kinda skinny in a short dress and long beads, a bell-shaped hat cocked over one ear and a big red flower pinned to it. He didn't necessarily incline toward skinny girls, but this one had great, sparkling eyes, and a wonder-smile on her painted mouth. She was hearing the music, no doubt there; hearing it and wanting to hear more.

She made for the empty table to the right of the stage. Her fella followed, but it was plain he wasn't best pleased; jerking his head toward the back o'the room, where there was an arm in the air. Bigger'n her, naturally; burly and thick muscled in a tailored suit; his hair was glossy with brilliantine, slicked back from a square, hard face. He had a little black mustache over a full red mouth, and his hands were square and soft.

He jerked his head again toward the back of the room. The girl pouted. Her fella pulled her chair out with ill-grace, and went to the back of the room alone.

Andy forgot about her for a while then, lost in the music himself. The next time he noticed her was during his supper break. Her fella had come back to her table and was apparently wanting to move on. The girl shook her head, and he grabbed her wrist, jerking her to her feet.

Andy came away from the bar fast, meaning to have a word with the boy, but—she looked right at him; met his eyes like she could see them behind the dark lenses. . .

. . .and shook her head.

He nodded, slightly, and went back to his supper, watching as her fella pulled her arm through his, and they moved toward the door. It seemed she went willing, and her fella stayed civilized, 'til they were out of his sight, gone into the breezy September night.

Andy sighed, still feeling unsettled, which was just foolishness. He didn't have nothing to do with people from Away. Nothing to do at all.

#

He amused himself with a run of old ballads: Low Bridge, Old Dan Tucker, Big Rock Candy Mountain—nobody noticed. Nobody ever did. He played 'til it was time to stop playing, got the guitar into its case, and drank a last beer while Flannagan counted out the hat. Two dollars and eighty-five cents; more than he'd expected from this crowd. He left fifty cents on the bar, so Mr. Flannagan wouldn't find him to be lacking in gratitude, stowed the rest in his pockets and strolled down the noisy, crowded room. The guy on the door opened up for him; he nodded his thanks, and followed the smoke out into the sweet autumn air.

#

He walked down the hill, among the glare of the electric lights. Despite the hour, the streets were crowded; the light spilling from the new hotels making the street as bright as day. Down at the bottom of the hill was the Pier, hung with so many lights it looked like a sun had fallen into the sea. Andy could hear the band playing at the Casino—Paul Whiteman's Orchestra, it was this weekend—nice and clear.

He ambled along, in no rush to be anywhere, guitar case over his shoulder, weighing whether he wanted to go over to the Casino and take in what was left of the show. Might learn something.

Or might not. He didn't much care for the Big Band sound, and while some of the arrangements might be adapted for a single fella and his guitar, most were built for that full orchestra.

Be a lot more to learn at the jam session, after the Pier closed down for the night and honest folk were asleep. That was when the roadies, and some of the orchestra musicians, too—the ones who lived the music almost like Andy did—they'd get together to play. Blues, now, there was something a fella and his guitar could learn from the Blues. Might be good to sit in, tonight. Nothing else doing, after all.

It was right about then that he noticed her, keeping pace with him on the crowded walk, a careful arm's length away.

Andy stopped. The girl stopped, too, and turned to face him. Her big eyes were bright under the brim of the perky little hat—bright and hard as glass. He could see her shivering, which was no surprise. September it might be, and mild, yet, but they were still on the Maine coast, and the wind off the ocean wanted a shawl or a jacket to turn it.

"Best you go inside," he told her, gentle, because it took some that way, those who really *heard* the music, and they got confused about what it was they wanted. "I've got nothing for you, missy."

"But you do." Her voice was husky, and it shivered, too. "Have something for me."

Well. Maybe he'd misjudged. He looked at her dress, the pearls, and the earrings. Expensive things, by his reckoning.

"You want money?" he asked.

"Money?" she repeated blankly, then swept her hand out, as if tossing the word, or a coin, away. "I don't care about money."

"Right, then. You go on back to your room, wherever you're staying."

Her hard, brilliant eyes widened, and she lunged, catching his sleeve.

"No!" she said sharply, and then, more moderately, "No, I can't go back there. Please—please walk with me, just down to the trolley stop."

They were blocking the sidewalk, or should've been. People flowed past without seeing them, no smallest shift of the eyes to acknowledge their presence. That was right, most folk didn't see him, unless he wanted them to, which he didn't, right at present, and they'd automatically look away from a girl who was talking to herself.

Still, seemed the best thing to do was ease off the don't-see-me, and get her out of the way before some drunk trampled her, or a fella with an eye to opportunity decided she was too crazy to know what was happening to her

"Sure," he said. "I'll walk you down. Best step it up; last trolley for Portland leaves at midnight."

"I know," she said, and, "thanks."

He waited for her to let go his sleeve, but she didn't, just stood there looking at him, shivering in the breeze—or maybe, he thought suddenly, not only with the breeze.

"Where's your fella?" he asked her.

She blinked. "Gone drinking with Percy. I told him I was tired, and wanted to go back to the hotel to sleep."

He nodded, and, when she still didn't move, or let go of him, he turned and started walking again, down the hill.

She went with him, drawing closer, and slipping her hand into the crook of his arm, like they were walking out together. That hurt, that did, and he almost pulled himself free of her.

"You can, can't you?" she said breathless and shaky before he could pull away. "You can. . .fix things."

He felt a thrill; a stronger repeat of the sensation he'd had earlier, that there was *something special* about. . .to happen. He'd seen that the girl heard the music; that she'd also been able to puzzle out the music's purpose—well. There were those who could see the wyrd and understand the strange, even though they, themselves, were neither.

Her question wanted answering, though, and he had to be careful with it.

"I can't fix anything," he said, and felt the sour truth in his belly.

"Not you, maybe," she said, talking fast, now; her words tumbling over each other like puppies. "The guitar—the *music*—that's it, isn't it? I felt it, back there in the bar. I felt it begin to—to stitch me together." Her laugh was even less steady than her voice.

"Stitch me together, that was it. Like a kid's ragdoll."

"Look, missy," he said. "Whatever you want—"

"I want you—the music—I want. . .to be fixed. It—the music—it can do that, can't it?"

She'd found the twist, bless the girl. *He* couldn't fix one blessed thing, true enough, but the music—that was something else.

Careful again, he said, "It can't *fix*. Not the way you're thinking, it can't." He hesitated, and threw her a glance.

That was a mistake. Her face was rosy, her eyes on fire; the bright red mouth pinched until it was hardly pink.

"What's the trouble?" he asked, the words drawn unwilling out of him, one by one.

"I just want to get away, that's all!" she said, her fingers digging into his arm like a vise. "But he has the stuff, and he—I—if I don't have it, I'll die."

He knew then, why her eyes was so bright, and why she shivered so.

"Your fella gives you dope?" he asked.

She nodded, jerkily.

"It was—swell at first, y'know? But it didn't stay swell. I'm sick of it—and I'm sick without it."

"That's how it goes with the dope," Andy said, and it was pity he felt for her, knowing now why she was so thin. "Nothing to fix it, that I ever heard."

"If I can get away," the girl said. "Go up to Portland. I got—I got an old school chum in Portland. She'll help me."

"Then you don't need me," he said. "Last trolley to Portland's at midnight."

"I know that, don't I? Or why'd I ask you to walk me to the stop?"

"You said you wanted to be fixed," he reminded her.

"Fixed—I need; I need to stay strong enough—to not go back—to get on that trolley and get to Sarah."

It wouldn't do her any good, and might hurt Sarah, too, depending on how deep the dope had a grip. Not his problem; he told himself. He had nothing to do with folks from Away.

He sighed, lightly, and put his hand over her fingers that were leaving bruises on his arm.

"I'll wait with you," he told her. "And I'll maybe play some while we wait."

Hope flared in those too-bright eyes.

"Thank—"

"No, now, hear me out! There's no fixing involved. Music might put a little courage in you, maybe. *Maybe*. And not so much as that." When she crossed out of Archers Beach—well, he didn't know what happened to the music's power, outside of Archers Beach, now did he?

"Courage enough to hold you on the trolley," he said, not promising it—not exactly. "So you'll sit tight, all the way into the city. Get a taxi to your friend. Understand me. . ." He paused, thinking how best to tell her that distance wasn't what she needed; that she was carrying her doom inside her—she was sick, he recalled her saying. Well, then, she knew as much as he did.

"Sylvia," she said, shaking him out of his thoughts.

He looked down into her face again.

"What?"

"Sylvia. It's my name."

He felt it strike him, solid, like a fist against the heart, and almost swore. Dammit, he hadn't asked for her name!

Asked or not; he had it, now. And everything that went with it.

He sighed.

"Dangerous thing to be giving your name out to anybody," he said, mild, like it made no difference.

"You're not anybody," she answered. A breath, and she added, "You don't have to tell me yours."

Damn right, he didn't have to tell her his.

"Cross here," is what he said, and took them across Archer Avenue, to Milliken.

"Trolley stops on Grand," Sylvia objected.

"Stops on Milliken first, and it's quieter there. You want the music to concentrate on you, right?"

She nodded, jerkily. "Right."

The town council had planted fewer street lights on Milliken, it being a secondary way. There was plenty of spill off of Archers Avenue, though, and a lamp post right next to the trolley stop, its light furry in the sea-damp air.

Andy settled into the corner of the little wooden bench, and slipped the guitar out of its case. He could feel the music buzzing in his fingers; buzzing in his head. It came on like that, sometimes, 'specially if he hadn't played in a while. After a night of moving music through him. . .it worried him a little, just while he was getting the case out of the way and settling his fingers along the strings. It worried him, that the music was so eager, almost like it. . .had a plan.

It ought to worry him, that the music had a plan, but once he had his fingers on the frets, nothing worried him at all.

"Sit on down," he murmured. "We got a couple minutes."

"I don't want to sit down!" she snapped, and he might've snapped back, but there wasn't any sense to it—it was the dope making her twitchy and mad.

"Suit yourself."

His fingers were already moving, teasing out a melody—Simple Gifts, it was. Good music, that one; gentle.

Powerful.

What it felt like, playing the music—the kind and style of music he played. . .It felt like. . .it felt like he went all still at the dead center of him while light filled him up, flowing out through his fingers to wash away the pain and sadness around him.

That was why he'd stopped playing, after Nessa married her prince and took herself off to the Land of the Flowers. He'd told her that he was happy, so long as she was happy—but that'd been a lie.

The truth was, it felt like his heart'd been torn out, and there was no still place inside him for the light to fill up. He'd gone back to his land, threw himself into its care and keeping, not thinking; only serving.

Until the night he found himself standing on the corner of Milliken and Archer, hat on the ground by his feet, his fingers bleeding from the strings—playing.

Playing.

That had hurt—the music melting the scar tissue; growing him a new heart. It had hurt for a long time, but he learned. He learned to let the music—what the music was and everything that it did—fill him up and flow away. It was his gift—his gift to give away.

It was rare that he played just for one person. The full power of the music focused on a single heart and soul—not many could bear that. When he'd been young, and learning his gift, he'd broken a man's heart, playing just to him. His fault; he hadn't known the limits of a human heart, then. Still didn't, though he had a far shrewder notion.

He learned to play for big groups; he'd learned to give the music away to the street, to a meadow, to the sea—and to those strong enough to bear it.

This girl now, this Sylvia—she was only human, wyrd-sighted though she seemed. Whole and healthy, she wasn't strong enough to bear the full brunt of the music; sick with the dope like she was, and dying—the best thing the music could do, to *fix* her, like she wanted, was to kill her outright, and stop her from hurting any more.

His fingers moved along the frets without him paying any particular mind, and it was Shenandoah this time, easing into the space that had been warmed by Simple Gifts. Andy looked up, wanting to see how she was bearing it—but what he saw was the music, swirling 'round and through her, lighting her up like she was a candle.

A funny kind of candle, with the flame guttering, and a space of blackness before there was light again, burning brilliant and brave.

He watched, his fingers moving up and down the strings; he watched the music coil around the brilliant base of the candle and. . .tighten. The light moved up, slow, like the dark patch was almost too heavy to budge.

The music tightened again. He found his fingers insistent, and it was some Spanish thing now, that he'd learned from that sailor, long winters ago. Flamenco, thrumming hard and insistent, exerting pressure, until, the white base of the candle flowed upward into the darkness, and the crowning flame flared bright blue-white.

The bottom half of the candle—that was dark, now, and Andy's fingers slowed, sliding out of insistence into a gentle murmur; not music, really; more like whistling to yourself when you'd just done something that scared you bad.

The music flowed away, the image of the candle faded, and it was just the girl, Sylvia, standing there and staring at him, her face a little pale now, and her eyes soft with tears.

"You fixed me," she whispered. "I felt—"

"You felt," he said, his voice a harsh counterpoint to the murmur of the music. "You felt half your life taken off the back end, and applied to the front. You won't die this week, missy, but you won't live out the length you was given."

Her mouth tightened, the lipstick long gone, and then she nodded, once, firmly enough that the brave red flower on her hat jerked with it.

"But I was *going* to die this week, wasn't I?"

"Can't say that, missy, but you were in a bad way."

"Then I'll take that shorter span," she said firmly, and stiffened her thin shoulders.

"What're you gonna do, then?"

"Like I said. Go to Portland; find Sarah. Figure out what to do with what I've got left."

A bell sounded, around a crackle of electricity.

Sylvia looked over her shoulder.

"The trolley's here," she said, but instead of moving toward the curb, she stepped up to the bench, leaned down and kissed his cheek.

"Thank you," she said. "I mean that."

She turned, then, took a step, turned back to look at him, a wry grin on her pale face.

"I don't have car fare."

He snorted lightly, and came to his feet, one hand still fondling the strings while he dug into his pocket and pulled out his evening's earnings.

"Here."

"That's too much!"

"Taxi ride to Sarah, once you're in Portland," he said. "Something to eat, maybe." He pushed the money at her. "I'll get more, tomorrow."

She laughed. "You talked me into it."

The trolley arrived with a clang of the bell, the door clattered open.

"Milliken Street!" the conductor yelled. "All aboard for Portland, Congress Street Car Barn!"

A fella came down the stairs, none-too-steady on his feet, tipped his hat in Sylvia's general direction—"Miss."—and charted an uncertain route down Milliken, taking the corner wide at Imperial, and heading up the hill, toward the boarding houses.

Sylvia mounted one step, and stopped to look over her shoulder at him.

"Come with me," she said.

He shook his head, both hands on the strings, and the music moving softly out into the night.

"Got everything I need, right here."

"Lucky you," she said.

"Hey!"

Andy turned, fearing the worst—and here it came, the fella she'd been with at The Conch, hatless and running.

"Sylvia! Hey! Hold that trolley!"

She froze; she half-turned. . .

"Jake?"

Andy brought his hand across the strings in a slash, waking discord.

"Go!" he shouted, and used what she'd freely given him against her.

"Sylvia! Get on the trolley!"

Her body stiffened. Wooden, but obedient to his command, she mounted the steps. The doors clashed shut behind her. Electricity crackled; sparks danced along the wire.

"Hey!"

The fella—Jake—slammed to a stop by the bench, breathing hard, and shaking his fist at the trolley's backside.

"Evenin', Jake," Andy said, quiet and firm.

The man turned toward him, eyes widening.

"You—What'd you do with my girl?"

"Gave her some help. She asked me."

"Yeah? Well, you're gonna be sorry you did that. How about I break that guitar over your head?"

"No," Andy said, and heard the music coming out of the guitar, thick and dark and heavy.

He tried to stop, but the music had him as much as it had Jake, and the music was *angry*.

"You better leave," he told Jake, and tried to change it; to play something else. He thought the notes of Simple Gifts; but his fingers continued to call forth darkness and doom. The strings were icy against his skin, and he saw the music flow into the man and through him.

Saw the candle—saw, Andy thought, the man's *soul*—dull and tarnished thing that it was, with its flame guttering orange.

His fingers were pitiless; they played on, and the dark music swept out in an eddy so poisonously perfect that Andy felt the tears prick his eyes.

There was no filling here; no squeezing, neither. Just a breeze, that was all, cold, and soft, and sudden.

The candle flame flickered, guttered. . .and licked back up, just a glow now. . .

Andy drew a breath; he drew deep, on all the power he had in him.

He lifted his hand away from the strings.

The music stopped.

The man's guttering soul flickered in the passing of the cold breeze; Jake swayed—then straightened as the flame steadied and flared..

"You. . ." he snarled again, taking a step forward.

Andy slashed his hand across the strings, making them scream.

"Run!" he shouted. "Jake, you better run away—and forget you knew Sylvia!"

He felt that last bit take, just before Jake jumped like he'd been poked with a hot wire. A harsh gasp, near enough to a scream, got loose from him, and his slick-soled shoes scraped the sidewalk as he sprang into a run, up Milliken, back toward the lights of Archers Avenue.

Andy watched until Jake was just one more silhouette among the many up on the Avenue. Then, he walked over to the bench and put his guitar away in its case.

He stood for a little while, then, shivering; the breeze off the ocean having gone from chilly to cold.

"Shows what comes of dealing with folks from Away," he said, to nobody in particular.

He sighed, and slung the case over his shoulder, looking toward home.

Midnight, he thought. The Big Band would be finishing up its last set real soon, and the jam session'd be warming up. He wanted voices around him, and music, that was what.

Tonight now, he thought, moving slow toward Archer Avenue. Tonight, he'd learn to play the Blues.

The night don't seem so lonely

"And that was Yellow Submarine by the fab four, also known as—THE BEATLES!" The DJ's voice evaporated into a cloud of static, and came back, a little watery now:

". . .listening to WKOX-FM, one-oh-five-point-seven, Framingham, Mass. All rock, all the—"

More static, fizzing loud.

"Jesus Christ!" Ben swore. "Find another station, willya, Mossie?"

Moss leaned forward, fiddling with the dial, picking up a lot of static, and a thin line of what might've been "Crystal Blue Persuasion," though it was hard to tell in the rush of road noise coming in the open windows.

He upped the volume just in time for the thread of song to dissolve into a loud honk of noise.

"Christ!" Ben swore again, his hand flashing out.

Moss ducked—not that Ben had hit him, yet—and the music clicked off.

"Goddamn dead zone," Ben said. "You wait'll we get to Portland. Got a stereo set up, all the records you can listen to: Beatles, Stones, Dylan, Doors—all the good stuff. You'll like it just fine."

Moss had heard this before—Ben had picked him up a couple miles south of the Mass Pike, so they'd been together almost a day. The story was that Ben shared a house in Portland, Maine, on India Street. The plan—Ben's plan—was for Moss to come home with him, and "help out" for crash space and food.

It was a nice plan, Moss thought—for Ben. He didn't particularly have anything against Ben, mind. The man'd been more than fair with him: fed him a couple burgers, with fries, made sure he had a new, cold Coke every time they stopped for gas, offered to share his cigarettes and his reefers, too; and had only wanted one blow-job, which he'd asked for, nice and polite. His momma would've liked Ben.

Well, and Momma never did have no sense in men; which was the reason Moss was sixteen, and hitchin', and givin' blow-jobs to such folk as might pick him up. Momma'd taught him it was wrong to be beholden, so he made sure him and his rides were caught up even by the time he left 'em.

. . .though that was lookin' like it might be a problem, with Ben, here. Moss had no intention of letting himself be took into a strange house in a strange city and set to work givin' blow-jobs—or worse—to them he owed nothing to—or maybe Ben had the idea he'd like to deliver reefers, which he wouldn't much care for, neither.

Trouble was, they were getting close to Portland—he'd seen a sign 'bout ten miles back that said 38 miles, which meant he was going to have to give Ben the slip at the next gas stop.

He glanced over at the dash. Gauge was showing under a quarter, and the way this old Lincoln drank down the gas, no way they were making even twenty-five more miles without a top-off.

"Be home for dinner," Ben said, maybe thinking he was looking at the odometer. "We'll stop and pick up some groceries—beer, Coke, whatever you like—'fore we get there. Sound good to you, Mossie?"

"Sure," he said, and smiled, because Ben would want him to smile and be excited about comin' inside to a regular house where there was a shower, and regular meals an' all. A place where he could be useful and maybe earn some money and not have to put up with Momma's new boyfriend whaling on him, and calling him a freak and a weakling, and yelling at him to *die, already*.

His momma—give her credit—she hadn't liked seein' her boyfriend smacking her sickly son around, so she'd done what she could, since she wasn't going to be givin' the boyfriend up no time soon, not with a new baby on the way. She'd given Moss his own daddy's backpack, from when he'd been in the Army, and she'd told him to pack up his clothes and any other little thing that was his. Then, she'd given him nineteen dollars, which was all the grocery money, drove him out to the edge of the city, so the cops wouldn't give him no hassle, opened the door and told him to go.

He gave her back a ten, because he knew she'd want to think well of herself, and remember that she hadn't sent him out empty-handed. The boyfriend, though, he'd still expect to eat, and there wasn't no sense her getting the man mad when she'd just done him a good turn.

She took the money quick enough that he knew she'd been counting on him giving some back. He picked up his pack from between his feet, and got out of the car.

"Moshe," she said, just as he was shutting the door.

"Ma'am?"

"You remember now—don't you walk too hard, or too far. You mind your heart. Promise me."

"I promise, Momma," he said, giving her a smile to show he didn't mind it; and closed the door nice and soft.

By the time he'd gotten to the end of the parking lot, she was gone.

"We'll pull over for gas just up the road," Ben said, breaking into his thoughts. "Get us some Cokes and chips to last the rest of the way."

Moss looked out the window, saw a long main street like a lot he'd seen in New England—hardware store, five and dime, diner. . .and 'way up the end of the block, on the right, a white, red and blue Esso sign.

"Where are we?" he asked, 'cause of course the hardware store was somebody's name, which wasn't no help, and the diner was The Golden Rooster, with a big sign in the front window that said, "Something to Crow About!"

"Saco," Ben said. "That bridge we just come across was the Saco River. Town just the other side was Biddeford."

"And next is Portland?"

"Nah. Still gotta do the rest of Saco, then Scarborough, then over the bridge into the city. Twenty miles, maybe. Home for dinner, just like I said."

This was definitely the place for him to get off.

Moss smiled. "Sounds great," he said.

Ben pulled up to the pumps, and cut the engine. Moss opened his door.

"Gotta hit the head," he said. He closed the door briskly and walked to the office.

"Key?" he said to the guy behind the counter.

"Over there on the hook," the guy said, jerking his head to the left without bothering to look around.

Moss snagged the one labeled "M" and was out the door, ducking past Ben as he came in, and scooting around the side of the building.

But he didn't go to the men's room. He tucked the key on its piece of wood in the back pocket of his jeans, and looked around the corner at the car.

There was only one guy on, and he'd put the pump on automatic while he got under the hood to check the oil.

Good, thought Moss. It was time to leave Ben and get on alone. He couldn't risk the house on India Street, not by a long damn, he couldn't. Sure, he was on the street, and he didn't have an address, but he'd talked to the other kids he'd met on his way out from KC. Some of 'em—a lot of 'em—they'd made mistakes, and they were willing to share what they'd done wrong, or seen done wrong, what and who to look out for. . .

He didn't quite have Ben figured, but that didn't matter. The only kind of person who picked up a hitcher, treated him good, and promised him a nice room in his own home—was the kind of person no hitcher wanted to know. Might be Ben was on good behavior until they got to that house, which might not even be his. Some places, after they had a kid for a while, they sent him out to get more kids. . .

Well.

Wasn't here nor there, really. He had a plan—he had a duty—and he was gonna see it done. He'd promised.

Moss slipped around the back of the car, opened the back door, ducked inside and grabbed the strap of his backpack.

Easing the door closed, he looked to the front, but the gas-guy was still fiddling around with the engine. He stood on tiptoes to look over the roof of the Lincoln; saw Ben in the window, talking with the office man, but shifting a little like Ben did when he was nervous. Might be he was starting to wonder how long Moss was gonna take.

Time to go.

He fished the key out of his back pocket and dropped it onto the tarmac, then slung the pack over his shoulder, ducking a little to be sure he was below the line of the car's roof, and angled toward the shrubs and trees lining the edge of the station.

He'd just gotten past the shrubs and was almost into the trees when he heard somebody running behind him, and Ben's voice yelling.

"Hey! Hey! Moss! You come back here, you little—Hey! Somebody help me catch that kid, he's got my wallet!"

That didn't take long.

Moss pushed further into the trees, wondering how deep the little wood was. Behind, there came some crashing and snapping as branches broke, and Ben yelling, "C'mon Moss, quit foolin' around; we gotta go!" and the gas guy maybe it was yelling, "C'mon, kid; the boss is calling the cops. Just throw the guy's wallet out here and everything's square."

"What the hell you talkin' about?" Ben yelled. "He's with me!"

"Thought he had your wallet."

"Well, he does. He. . .plays these jokes. But we're together. Mossie! C'mon, it ain't funny no more."

No, thought, Moss, it wasn't. Up ahead, flashing silver through the leaves, he saw a chain link fence. Behind him, they were still crashing, and to the right. . .

To the right, it was downhill and more trees and maybe he could lose them, if he ran like hell.

#

He dropped to his knees in a little clearing, panting for air and his heart pounding funny like it did, and there were little spikes of pain in his chest, and he just put his palms flat against the dirt, and hoped that this wasn't it, the time that his bad heart went bust on him, and then he hoped that it was, it hurt so bad, and then. . .

. . .he woke up to the soft inquiry of an owl, and stars above him, between the leaves. He was tired, but nothing hurt, and he took a deep breath of the cool, damp air, tasting salt.

The ocean, that must be. He was close to the ocean—the Atlantic Ocean, that was. He'd struck out deliberate for the Atlantic Ocean, all those weeks ago, on account of his duty. His promise to his dad. 'course, his dad'd thought—had said!—that Moss would make good on the promise when he was a man.

Wasn't dad's fault that Moss wasn't likely to live that long. He hadn't caught the fever 'til after dad was gone himself. Strep throat, that was what they thought. . .

Well.

Water under the bridge. His dad used to say that. *That's just water under the bridge, Moshe, all flowed away and gone.*

That was what happened to the bad things—they all flowed away, to the ocean, and the ocean salt dissolved them. Try to carry the bad things around, and they'd weigh you down into the ground.

The good things, though, you carried them with you, 'cause good things, they didn't weigh no more than sunlight.

The owl hooted again, softer, like maybe it was telling him to go back to sleep; he was safe here.

Moss took another deep breath, smiling at the lack of pain.

Tomorrow, he thought drowsily, he'd find the ocean.

#

The sand on the beach was just like his dad had told him, white, like snow; fine as flour. Surely was pretty, but it was tricky to walk in. His sneakers were sliding and his knees were working, and it was hard to make any headway. He did it, though he was panting like a grampaw, and his heart was kinda beating strange, one thump harder than the next two. No pain, though, so he didn't mind it, much.

What his dad hadn't told him about, though, was how the air smelled—not just salty, but fresh, like air right after a thunderstorm. Smelling it made him feel like dancing, though maybe not in the dry sand.

Finally, he made it to wet sand. He could walk better now, almost like on a sidewalk, and he kept on going, to where the waves come in, rolling soft and slow, and every one that found the sand making a sweet little *plash*.

Moss stood there, looking out over the bright, glittery, gently rolling waters, and he felt something happen in his chest—not pain, or that squeezing thing that sometimes happened. No. . .it felt, somehow like he was happy—too happy to laugh.

So happy, his stupid heart wanted him to cry.

Well. . .

He slung the pack around and lowered it to the sand, then knelt and undid the buckle.

There, in the hidden pocket underneath the right back pocket, he found the little pouch, and pulled it out.

For a long time, they'd just sat out on a shelf in his room, but when Momma's new boyfriend moved in, Moss had thought maybe it would be better to empty his old shooters out into his sock drawer, and put his dad's tokens into the bag, outta sight.

The bag, he tucked under his t-shirts, and the boyfriend never found it to break, though he'd broken some other stuff he had no business putting his hands on...

Moss closed his eyes and took a breath.

Water under the bridge, he told himself, *all flowed away and gone.*

Leaving the pack where it was, he walked down to the place where the little waves kissed the beach. There were shells, here and there on the wet sand; strings of weed, and stones as shiny as living eyes.

Just by his foot were two flat, round bones, beige-brown and laying together in the damp. *Sand dollars,* they were called, his dad had told him, on account they looked like big ol' silver dollars. The two on the beach were damp, and gritty with sand, and though they looked stiff, he knew that they were living critters.

The one he took outta his pouch, though, that one was white as bone, the critter long dead. He put it on the wet sand near the two live ones, and then reached into the bag for the couple other shells, scattering them onto the sand from his fingertips as he walked a little ways down the waterline.

When the bag was empty, he upended it, so any sand and grit and pieces could fall out, then shoved it into his pocket.

He took a deep breath, looking out over the water, and sighed.

Duty done. Promise kept. The lazy, rolling water glittered a little more, like maybe he'd caught some drops on his eyelashes.

Another breath, and here came a roller that was taller than the others, seeming to move a little faster, too. Before he could figure out how that might be, it struck the sand with a *boom!* White spray flew into the air, splashing his face, then the wave was gone, leaving Moss with his jeans wet and his sneakers soggy. The sand around him, where he'd left the shells and the dead sand dollar, was clean, just like somebody had reached out a hand and swept them off the beach.

* * *

"Here he comes back, now," Felsic said, leaning on the ticket counter under Noah's Ark.

Phyllis didn't bother to look up from her newspaper.

"Lost boy from Away got nothing to do with me. *Or* with you."

"Might be he's not lost," Felsic said; "that's what's nagging at me."

Phyllis rattled the paper.

"Says here, next month, NASA's gonna be trying to land on the moon. Think o'that, now, eh?"

"Quite an age we live in," Felsic said agreeably.

The boy'd been down to the sea; his jeans was wet to the knee, and his sneakers squelched on the land. Might've made an offering—he had the look of it. Gone down heavy, come back light. Wasn't nothing more keeping that boy from floating off to the moon his own self, now that the sea'd taken what he'd brought to it.

"Hungry," Felsic said, because Phyllis wasn't near as cold as she talked, and she was listenin', even if she was pretendin' not to be lookin'.

"Give 'im a job," Felsic urged; "can't hurt."

Phyllis sighed gustily, rattled the paper closed, and stared across the parking lot at the kid an' his backpack an' the dazed way he was starin' around.

"All right," she snapped. "I'll give 'im a job, if he wants one, but I ain't chasing 'cross the parkin' lot to hand it to 'im. He gets his tail over here like a sensible boy, and looks at the board, then—all right."

"Fine," Felsic said soothingly. "That's fine."

A little ripple, that's all it took, the boy might be from Away, but he wasn't one o'the deaf-and-blind ones. No, he felt the ripple, took the suggestion into his head, and started moving 'cross the lot, toward the Ark, and the signboard over at the side saying *Operators Wanted*.

Phyllis saw him moving, took note of his direction and turned a pretend glare on Felsic.

"Well, *boss*?" she asked, sarcastic, but that was just her way. "Where you puttin' him?"

"Jack 'n Jill," said Felsic promptly. "Sally'll do 'im a world o'good."

* * *

Sally was a little bit something: She teased, and laughed, climbed up the outside scaffolding like a cat, expecting him to keep up. His momma would've said she was "lively." Moss thought she might be something more—or other—than just that. Her eyes flashed yellow in the shadow sometimes, like cat-eyes. She slipped a little, climbing ahead of him, and he thought he saw claws come out from the tips of her fingers and snag the canvas awning stretched between the slide and Noah's Ark.

Still and all, he liked her—claws and cat-eyes, too. She'd come back down the scaffold to him when he'd had to rest in his climb, an' asked what was the matter.

"Little breathy; need a quick rest. I got a tricky heart," he told her, which was more than he told most people, for fear of being laughed at. "Had rheumatic fever when I was a little kid."

"That mean you shouldn't climb?" she asked. "'cause, if you want, we can just set you down at the gate t'take admission. I can do what climbing needs done."

There now—*that* was why he liked her. She didn't make fun, and she didn't disbelieve, or go tell Boss Phyllis he was *sick*, either; just offered up a plan for how to work the ride out between 'em.

"I can climb; just sometimes I gotta rest."

"OK, then," she said, and perched on the bar above him, easy as a cat, until he started cilmbing again.

Up at the top of the slide, standing on the platform, you could see everything there was to see in Archers Beach and beyond—the sun glittering on the ocean, and the land curving, miles away. He could see it all, despite the glittery sea and the fresh damp air making his eyes water. Sally got him turned around so he could look up the hill at the stores and the people shopping, and the cars and delivery trucks doing business.

"This is my favorite place," Sally said, close in his ear, like she was telling him a secret. You can see *every*thing."

Well, you couldn't see Kingman, Kansas, but maybe that was all right, too. Moss took a deep, deliberate breath of wonderful air, and smiled.

"Sure is fine," he said, and Sally laughed.

"Where're you from?"

"Kansas," he said. Sally frowned like he'd said something foreign.

"Much like here?" she asked.

"Not anything like here."

"What brings you to us, then?"

He shook his head, his eyes damp from the sun striking off all that moving blue water.

"Made a promise to my dad. He was here, years back. Picked up some shells and stuff on the beach. He gave 'em to me, before he died, and said that I had to go to Archers Beach when I was grown up, and give the shells back to the sea. Made me promise. So, I come to fill the promise."

Sally didn't make a fuss about that, either, or tell him he was silly. He had the feeling that Sally took promises serious, and he liked her even more.

"Be going back soon?"

Going back? thought Moss. What would he go back for? Or to?

He shook his head.

"I think I'll stay here. I think. . .my dad wanted me to see something different. He told me how, when he first saw the Atlantic Ocean, he said it changed his whole life, and how he saw the world."

"He went back, though," Sally said, looking down at the parking lot below them.

"He did, yeah. He'd made his own promise, that he would go back. He was married to my mother."

Sally nodded, still staring down.

Moss looked up, into the deep blue sky. A shadow flashed over his face, and a seagull screamed. Music started from somewhere—sounded like merry-go-round music.

"We gotta get down," Sally said. "Park's opening for the day."

He did look down, then, thinking about the climb before him, and trying to guess would his chest seize again, like it'd done on the way up.

"We'll take the easy way down," Sally said, picking up a rough-wove mat, and dropping it flat to the platform.

"Here," she said.

Moss blinked.

"Sit down!"

She sounded a little impatient, suddenly, so he dropped to the mat—and gasped when she hit him between the shoulder blades. He yelled, the mat skidded forward, tipped—and hit the slide.

Wind rushed past his ears as the mat picked up speed. He yelled again, and the rushing air snatched his voice away with the rest of his breath, and he was flying, flying toward the ground in a grand, speeding spiral, and he leaned in the next curve, deliberately increasing his speed, chest aching, and the salty breeze in his mouth, and there was the end of the slide, and a stocky figure in a cap at the end of it, and just beyond a pile of sawdust, and he was airborne, sawdust erupting in a fragrant cloud. He collapsed, gasping, until strong arms came around and half-dragged him up and away.

"Can't stay there, boy; we got incomin'," somebody—Felsic—said, propping him up against a sturdy shoulder. He heard a yell over the laboring bellows of his heart and here came Sally, her mat already airborne, and she was out, over the edge, hitting the sawdust and waking an explosion. Pine scent enveloped him and he coughed, grabbing at his chest, and it was glorious, and it hurt. . .it hurt. . .

. . .nothing hurt at all.

He was laying on the ground, in the shade next to the end of the slide. His head was on Sally's knee, and Felsic was bent over him, one hand on his chest, he *didn't* hurt anymore, but only kind of light and cool.

"What's the matter with you, deah?" Felsic murmured.

Moss tried to marshal words out of the vast sense of cool peace, but Sally was quicker.

"He said he's gotta tricky heart," she said. "Needed a breather, part way up, climbin'."

"Rheumatic fever," Moss managed, so they had the right name of it. And if it meant that he couldn't work here, couldn't stay here, then he'd *rather* die—

"Don't fatch," Felsic said, and Moss felt the rising panic reverse, and just drain away.

"That's it," Felsic said. "You rest a spell. Sal—you go open up. Moss'll be along shortly."

"All right," she said, and Moss felt lips, cool and slightly damp, pressed against his cheek, before she moved his head from her lap to something else soft, and he heard her sneakers scuffing on the tarmac.

"I can work," Moss said, though without any urgency. "Don't want the boss mad at me, right off."

"She's fine." Felsic leaned back, hand slipping into a pocket. "This heart business. . ."

"Means I'm gonna die. But not today."

"Well, then. That's all any of us got, ain't it? You sit up all right?"

He did, with Felsic's help, and a couple minutes later, he stood under the same conditions.

"I'm good," he said. "I can work."

Felsic nodded and stood.

"Up to Sally, o'course, but don't be surprised you're on ticket-box today."

"If that's were she needs me. . ."

A gong sounded, loud; somewhere nearby a mule brayed in either complaint or approval.

"That's my call to the Coal Mine. You go on, an' be good, right?"

"Right."

#

The rides closed at eight o'clock. Moss went to get his pack from where he'd stowed it, in Boss Phyllis' office.

"Sally said you did good today," the boss said. "You comin' back tomorrow?"

"Yes, ma'am. I'll come every day you need me."

She gave him a once-over at that, like she heard what he hadn't said, but all she said was, "Showers in the White Way, next door. You hungry, you stop at Bob's over at Grand and Dube and tell 'em behind the counter that you work for me. Same thing tomorrow breakfast."

Moss looked at her careful.

"That's included in, or comes outta my pay?"

"Included in. That *all right* by you, deah?"

"Yes, ma'am," he said again; added, "thank you, ma'am;" grabbed his pack and headed for the showers.

#

There was space for him at the counter at Bob's. He told the counterman he worked for Phyllis, and pretty quick a hamburg platter and a big Coke landed in front of him. He ate it all, even the lettuce, and was finishing up his Coke when he noticed somebody at his elbow.

Well, the placed as packed, and it was probably somebody wanted his place. Moss swallowed the last of his Coke and stood up.

"Sorry," he said—and right then recognized Felsic.

"Evenin'," Felsic said. "You have a good day at work?"

"I did. I like it. Boss said I can come back tomorrow."

"Phyllis likes an eager worker. You keep eager, and she'll keep happy. You mind if I walk a ways with you?"

Moss hesitated, looking at Felsic. He didn't get the feeling that this was a set-up, but. . .

"Just a walk down the beach," Felsic said, nice and easy. "I'll keep m'hands in m'pockets."

It came to Moss that he liked Felsic, and there wasn't really no harm going for a walk.

"Sure," he said.

#

"You got a place to stay?"

That was a dangerous question, even if he *did* like Felsic. He wanted to stay here, in Archers Beach. Might be he was tired; he'd pushed himself hard the last couple days, and it could be his heart was tired. He'd think that, 'cept he didn't feel tired at all.

He felt more alive than he'd ever had, in all his life.

"I don't got a place, right yet," he said, not wanting to outright lie.

"That's all right," Felsic said. "The land hereabouts is welcoming. You just find someplace comfortable and set down roots, if you've a mind to."

Moss considered that as they walked up the beach. The sand strip was much skinnier now, the sound of the waves striking a constant thunder in his ears. His bones shook with it.

Sally had told him that the water changed—the tide came in and the tide went out, but he hadn't been, in any way, prepared for the reality of high tide. The thunder and the spray and the salt and the wind—all of it just made him feel like shouting and dancing and take the thunder into his bones. . .

He closed his eyes and made himself pay attention to what Felsic had said.

"Just any place at all?" he asked. "Right here on the beach?"

"That could be a problem," Felsic said; "Generally the beach's held to be neutral—not belonging to the sea or the land, if you understand me."

Moss nodded.

"No man's land."

There was a small silence, then Felsic outright laughed.

"That's it, that's it, exact! No man's land! You go a couple blocks inland, you might find something that'll do. Otherways, there's a youth hostel up at the top of Walnut. They'll spot you a night, you tell 'em you're working for Phyllis."

"Thanks," Moss said.

"No trouble, no trouble at all. I get off here." Felsic nodded toward the board walk crossing the dunes back onto the streets.

"I'll come with you, if I can," Moss said.

"Nothing stopping you that I see," Felsic answered easily, and so they crossed the boards together, and together they walked down to Grand, where Felsic turned right. Since he didn't have any reason to go left or right, so Moss stayed with Felsic. There was something. . .not *kind*—No, thought Moss, definitely *not* kind—about Felsic. Comforting. Down to earth, that was it.

Moss decided that he liked Felsic very much, indeed.

They walked for two blocks, then Felsic angled across the street to a place that was nothing but two houses, backing on what smelled like a salt marsh.

"This is me," Felsic said, and reached out to touch him, softly on the arm.

"Try for something further in. Don't wanna walk too far to work."

That made sense, Moss thought, and in the time it took him to think so, Felsic had walked around the back of one of the houses—and was gone.

Moss shivered, though it was plenty warm.

Just went in the back door, he told himself, and as if to bear him out, a light came on in the nearest house.

Moss nodded, shifted his pack on his back and turned back toward the heart of town.

#

He didn't much care for the idea of staying at anything called a "youth hostel." There were a number of bad things that routinely happened in dormitories, a couple of which he'd experienced up close and personal. The worst part of those being that he'd known better.

Well, it wasn't raining fit to drown a frog tonight. Tonight it was fine and clear, and there weren't too many people around, down this part of town. No reason for people to come down this way, which didn't offer no music, nor beer, nor nothing much at all, 'cept some little houses, like where Felsic lived. Back one street, there were trees and marsh.

He hit the corner and paused. From the left, he heard the crash and thunder of the waves against the shore. His feet turned, just slightly in that direction, and then—

It smelled like green leaves, and clean dirt, and pine, with a sweet underneath—maybe some flower he didn't know. From his right, away from the sea, borne on a breeze, was what he thought, but the wind was coming from the left, damp and fresh off the back of the waves.

Moss breathed in, letting the sweet, green air melt in his mouth like ice cream. He thought of laying himself down on a mound of pine needles, and sleeping safe and unmolested.

He turned right, away from the crash and boom of the ocean, following the promise as much as the scent. A couple feet down, he left the sidewalk, following a thin, faintly glowing trail, through weeds and reeds, past some sapling trees, between a green-glowing boulder and a white birch tree. . .

. . .and into a clearing floored with soft pine needles. Just off center of the clearing stood the remains of a big, old tree, its limbs broken, but its trunk intact. He saw the small wrinkled objects dangling from one of the partial low branches, and put a name, at last, to the sweet smell.

Apples.

He sighed, looked around, feeling the welcome come up from the ground through the soles of his feet, and tears came to his eyes, even as he thought that this was what Felsic must've meant, about the land being welcoming.

And this little piece of land, right here, welcomed *him*.

"Thank you," he said, not feeling the littlest bit silly about talking outloud to trees and stones. "I'd like to stay here. I gotta get up in time for breakfast and work tomorrow, but I'll stay here, if you'll have me." He looked around, and saw the gleam of one of those stupid pull-tabs among the pine needles.

"I'll clean up," he said, "and do what else needs done."

The scent of apples grew momentarily stronger; he yawned, hard on it, and slipped his pack off his back.

"It's been a long day," he told the trees, and cast about him. There was a soft mound of leaves and old needles just under the old apple tree, and it came to him that there would be a comfortable bed.

He settled in with a sigh, his pack under his head, pine needles and dead leaves for a blanket, and drifted off to sleep.

#

He woke to bird song; opened his eyes and just laid there, smiling up into the broken branches above him and just feeling. . .happy. He'd had a dream that he'd talked to the grandmother of this little place, and she had told him that she loved him, and he could stay here forever, if he chose it.

Forever. Now, wasn't that something?

Moss sighed, and the bird sang again, louder this time, or so it seemed to Moss, and he remembered that he had to get up and go to work.

He left his pack leaning against the trunk of the old apple tree, confident that no one would mess with it while he was gone, then he left his welcoming little piece of land, and headed down to Bob's for breakfast.

#

He was at Noah's Ark well before the ten o'clock opening. Felsic was already there, tending the mules at the Coal Mine. Moss went over to help.

"Sleep good, deah?"

Moss smiled.

"Best in years. Found a. . .welcoming spot."

"Did you now?" Felsic murmured, moving a brush slowly down a mule's short neck.

Moss braced himself, but Felsic didn't ask him where he was sleeping. They finished up combing and harnessing in companionable silence, broken at last by the clang of the side gate closing.

"That'll be Sally," Felsic said. "Best you learn set-up over at the slide. 'preciate the help, here; you got a good hand with the animals."

"My grampaw had mules at his place. I used to help with 'em."

"Well, he taught you good. Go 'long, now."

#

It was good to belong, it was good to work, and to earn money, and to have a good, safe place that was his to care for, and that cared for him back. Summer heated up, people kept on coming down to Archers Beach, 'til there wasn't hardly any room to walk on the sidewalks, and the rides were busy from opening to close; and on July Fourth, him and Sally, and Felsic and Phyllis all climbed up to the top of Jack 'n Jill and stood on the platform to watch the fireworks. They were so high up, it was like being inside the sparks, and Moss felt each explosion echo in his chest.

In between, he worked on his land, clearing out the old trash, and finding the boundaries of the place that welcomed him, in particular, and bloomed under his care.

He met a bunch of folk, who worked on the rides, and elsewhere 'round the Beach. In particular, he met Vornflee, who was a friend of Felsic's, and who worked at the Moon Ride; and Bonny, who ran the carousel on the other side of the parking lot. Bonny was an important lady, Moss could see that. Even Phyllis deferred to her. She considered him for a long time after they was introduced, face serious; then she nodded, and put a hand on his shoulder.

"You'll do fine," she told him. "Just remember not to be afraid."

Truth said, he didn't have time to be afraid, busy as he was, and it was only 'cause Sally said something about the moon landing coming right up that he realized a month and more had gone past and he'd never been happier in his life.

"I'm goin' up to the top of the slide tonight, and see if I can't see it."

"See what?" Moss asked. "Moon's only just past new."

"The spaceship," Sally told him, with that little sniff that meant she was annoyed.

"Oh," Moss said, 'cause he didn't like Sally to be mad with him; "the spaceship. That's a different proposition. Maybe you *can* see that."

"I'm gonna try it," Sally said, determinedly; and added, with a side-look at him. "You can come up, too, if you want."

"Sure," he said. "Meet after dinner?"

She nodded, and the gong went off, and it was time to get to work.

#

He was finishing up his clam chowder when he heard the first siren, and lifted his head, eyes wide.

"Engine number one," Vornflee said, tipping his head, burger held between two hands.

"Headin' down the hill," Felsic said, pushing back from the table, and standing. "Let me just step outside an—"

"Fire at the White Way!" Bob yelled, coming out from the kitchen. "Just heard it on the scanner! All callmen wanted!"

Chairs scraped, and people jumped up, heading towards the door in a rush. Felsic started that way, too.

"You ain't a call man," Vornflee said.

"Fire at the White Way," Felsic said. "I better see to the mules."

Moss stood, too.

"I'll help," he said.

Vornflee sighed, put his burger down on the plate and got up, too.

"I'll watch."

#

There was a pumper engine 'round back of the White Way, and two volunteer firemen using hoses on a small, smoky fire at the back corner. Moss followed Felsic 'round and over the fence, which was a quicker route to the Mine—and 'sides none of them had the key to the gate.

The space between the rides was filled with smoke, and Moss could hear the mules calling.

"Open the gate," Felsic told Vornflee. "Moss 'n me'll get the animals."

Vornflee nodded and ran; Moss followed Felsic.

The smoke was thicker by the entrance to the Mine, swirling around like it knew there was live things inside for it to torment. Felsic opened the door to the mule pen.

"Get the old man," Felsic said, and Moss grabbed a halter from the wall and went over the fence. The mules were anxious. A couple of the youngers brayed, presssed against the back of the enclosure, like they were trying to get away from the smoke that stalked them even there.

Old Man, though, he saw Moss and moved forward, two more mules following. Moss got the halter on, and patted the old mule.

"Let's go. s'only smoke so far, but you keep sensible, in case you see any fire." He looked at the two keeping pace, though they had no halters: Lacey and Gretel, both sensible folk.

"C'mon, then," he said, and walked them out of the enclosure, into the waiting area, and out into the park.

The smoke was still swirling, and Moss coughed as it got into his mouth. The Old Man was coming right along and his friends, too. Ahead, through the smoke, Moss could see the park gate open, and the parking lot full of cars beyond. He could hear music, from the Pier, and people shouting.

Bonny from the carousel was waiting outside, with Phyllis. Bonny took the Old Man's halter and led him away, toward the beach, Gretel and Lacy still following. Moss turned back, and here came Felsic, the rest of the mules following behind.

"Beach," said Phyllis, and Felsic turned that way.

An explosion rocked the night; smoke belched out of everywhere, like the sidewalks had opened up and hell was coming forth.

"Pull back, pull back! She's going up!"—that was the guys in the pumper truck, and there were other guys yelling—"Get those cars outta here!" and the sound of breaking glass, and—"Oh, no," Phyllis whispered. "Sally."

Moss spun, staring up, and there, silhouetted against the rising flames, Sally stood on the topmost platform of the giant slide, looking out over the confusion, illuminated and then cast into shadow by the dancing flames.

The fire was everywhere, now. The pile of sawdust at the bottom of the slide was afire. The Moon Ride was hidden in smoke, and long threads of flame licked out of the entrance into Noah's Ark.

Moss threw himself at the scaffolding, starting to climb.

"Sally!" he yelled.

"Moss!"

"Climb down!"

"The slide!"

"The sawdust is on fire! Climb down!"

His chest was burning, which wasn't a surprise, with everything else on fire. He hung onto the scaffolding and looked up. Sally was climbing down. That was good. Sally climbed like a cat; he didn't worry about her falling, but if the scaffold got too hot to hold. . .

"Hey, you kids! Get outta there! Charlie! We need the hose!"

Water began to fall though the cloud of smoke. Moss clung and coughed, and watched Sally climb closer, and finally come to rest next to him.

"Why are they spraying us with water?"

"To keep the fire off of us," Moss gasped. "C'mon, we gotta get outta here."

#

It was gone.

They'd stood there, all together, their arms around each others' waists, watching the amusement park burned.

Around ten o'clock Noah's Ark screamed like a live thing, foundered and collapsed in on itself, flames shooting out of the crater left behind.

Soon after, Jack 'n Jill, girders and slide all soft and black, sagged, crashed to its knees, and tipped over onto its side. The Moon Ride was gone by then, and the White Way was nothing more than ash and glowing timbers.

More fire trucks had arrived from the towns nearby, and they mostly concentrated on keeping the fire from reaching the Pier. They ran hoses into the sea, sprayed down the charred entrance ramp, and managed to keep the fire on land. There were people on the Pier, stranded for now, though Moss thought they'd be able to get off fine—tomorrow, maybe, after they'd gotten boats in and the last of the fire had died.

For now, he was tired. His chest ached, a little, his throat was raw, and his eyes streaming. At last somebody—maybe it was Bonny, maybe it was Phyllis—got them moving, away from the destruction, down Grand, to Bob's.

The place was jammed, even more than usual, no place to sit, and Moss finally sort of leaned up against the wall, feeling empty and sad. It was so crowded, it was hard to breathe, and his head was thumping hard, in an irregular rhythm that was making him sick to his stomach.

Air, that was what he needed. No, more than that. He needed to go back to his place, his little piece o'land, and sit down under the broken apple tree. Maybe take a nap. . .

He pushed away from the wall, but—funny thing; his knees just wouldn't hold him and down he went, hitting a chair and making a big noise, an even bigger noise than what was happening in his head, and—

"Moss!"

Felsic, that was; Felsic picking him up and holding him like he didn't weigh nothing at all.

"Gotta get home," he said—or tried to say—"I don't feel so good."

"Where's home, Mossie?" That wasn't Felsic, that was Bonny, and it was Bonny's hand, he thought, that came cool across his forehead.

"Down on Walnut, little place, old apple tree. . ."

"*That* place?" Phyllis sounded startled, but from a long, long ways away. He was so tired. . .

"Easy, easy. . ." Felsic murmured.

He felt a little jolt of cool peacefulness, and things come nearer again, though there was something funny happening with his eyes.

"Boy's accepted," Vornflee said, and Bob's voice came in over that, with—

"The kid's dying, Bonny. . ."

"Perhaps not," Bonny said. "Felsic?"

"I'll carry him." He felt himself lifted and shifted and put his head against something firm and soft.

"You stick with me," Felsic whispered in his ear, or maybe straight into his head. "Stick with me, Mossie; I'll get you home."

#

Might've been he blacked out, 'cause the next thing he did know was the welcome of his own place, rising up into him. He smiled, and he was so very tired. . .

"Moshe, listen to me." That was Bonny again, calling him by his right name, which he'd rather she didn't. He was Moss now, and he belonged to this place.

"That's right," Felsic said. "But you gotta choose it, brother. The land won't take—you gotta give."

"Dying," Moss said, remembering Bob, and his heart, and his promise to his Momma, that he'd be careful—but he had been careful, just not. . .careful enough.

"Dying," Felsic said; "but not dead. If you choose it, the land will have you. But not even the land can cure the dead."

"Moss—" Bonny again. "Open yourself up to the land. It knows you, this land; it loves you. Give yourself to it. I'll tell you; I knew the lady who lived in that apple tree; I was only a sapling myself when she bent down to disease, but I remember her. She was a stickler, and she didn't love easy, but once she did, her heart never closed. If what's left of her in this land chose you, then you can't do any better."

"How. . ." The thumping, and his breathing. . .

"Felsic," Phyllis said. "Let him go. It's his choice now, and you've kept him overlong, if his choice is to go."

Go? But he never wanted to go! He wanted to stay right here, here with this sweet place that loved him and kept him safe—that he loved and would shield with his life and more—he'd promised!

"And I promised," said a voice that he knew better than his own.

He opened his eyes, and there she was, the grandmother of this place. She opened her arms, and he walked into her embrace.

He felt the welcome rise in him, like the tide; he smelled fresh green leaves and sweet apples, pine, and leaf mold, and it seemed, for a minute that his heart stopped beating altogether, and he didn't need breath at all. He felt the weight of the apple tree; knew the flowers like they were his own fingers, and the stones like they were his toes. He was Moss; he was the lady of the apple tree; and the little brown bird—the skylark—that sung him awake every morning, so he'd be on time for work. He was all of the pieces, and the perfect sum of everything. . .

"Here he comes back to us," Felsic said.

Moss opened his eyes, and smiled; feeling his land smile through him.

"I'm not going to die," he said, like he was comforting Felsic.

"Not for a good, long while, I'm thinking," Felsic answered, and all around him he heard an exhale as if a roomful of folk had suddenly sighed at once in relief and pleasure.

"Are we all. . .like this?" he asked, looking from face to face around him.

"We all have taken service with the land," Bonny said briskly. "Each in our own way."

"'cept Sally," said Vornflee.

"Sally's a cat," Moss said. "Even I know that."

"That's right," Felsic said. "Now, how're you feeling, brother Moss?"

Moss laughed, and sat up, full of energy and delight. He felt a chipmunk run light over the land, pine cone in his mouth, and grinned.

"Thank you," he said, to all of them gathered, and those others, who were listening in through their own connection to a piece of land, or a slice of marsh, or a rock, or a tree. He could. . .almost. . .see them all, behind his eyes. Soon, he'd sort them out.

"You okay with this, Moss?" Felsic asked him, and Moss laughed again.

"I'm home," he said; "and I ain't never leaving. Hard to be any more okay than that."

About the Author

Sharon Lee is the author of a contemporary, Maine-based fantasy trilogy set in the only slightly fictional town of Archers Beach: *Carousel Tides, Carousel Sun,* and *Carousel Seas,* published by Baen Books and available in trade paper, electronic and audiobook editions. She has also written two Maine-based mystery novels—*Barnburner* and *Gunshy*—and numerous shorter stories.

Both of the short stories in this echapbook are set in Archers Beach. A previous echapbook—*Surfside*—contains two more Archers Beach short stories.

In addition to her solo work, Sharon has co-authored 23 novels of science fiction and fantasy with her husband, Steve Miller. Nineteen of those works are set in their bestselling Liaden Universe® series.

Sharon lives in Maine with her husband, four cats, and rather a number of books. You can keep up with her through The Blog Without a Name at sharonleewriter.com.

Other Works by Sharon Lee

Saltation
Mouse and Dragon
Ghost Ship
Dragon Ship
Necessity's Child
Trade Secret
Dragon in Exile
Alliance of Equals (forthcoming in 2016)
LIADEN UNIVERSE® SHORT STORY COLLECTIONS
A Liaden Universe Constellation: Volume 1
A Liaden Universe Constellation: Volume 2
A Liaden Universe Constellation: Volume 3
THE FEY DUOLOGY
Duainfey
Longeye

The above novels, published by Baen Books, are available wherever books are sold, in paper, electronic, and audio editions

The short story collections are available in paper and ebook editions

For more Lee and Miller titles please visit Pinbeam Books: visit www.pinbeambooks.com

Don't miss out!

Click the button below and you can sign up to receive emails whenever Sharon Lee publishes a new book. There's no charge and no obligation.

https://books2read.com/r/B-A-MRWB-BVIG

BOOKS 2 READ

Connecting independent readers to independent writers.

www.ingramcontent.com/pod-product-compliance
Lightning Source LLC
Chambersburg PA
CBHW021939170626
46807CB00007B/3192